Pete the Cat

Firefighter Pete

HARPER FESTIVAL
An Imprint of HarperCollinsPublishers

by James Dean

HarperFestival is an imprint of HarperCollins Publishers.

Pete the Cat: Firefighter Pete
Text copyright © 2018 by James Dean and Kimberly Dean
Art copyright © 2018 by James Dean
Pete the Cat is a registered trademark of Pete the Cat, LLC.
All rights reserved. Printed in the United States of America.
Library of Congress Control Number: 2017942892
ISBN 978-0-06-240445-9

20 21 22 CWM 10 9
❖
First Edition

"**W**e are going on a class trip today," says Principal Nancy.

She leads the class to a bright yellow bus. Everyone climbs on board.

"I wonder where we are going," says Pete.

They are going to visit the Firehouse today!
The bus parks next to the bright red Firehouse.
Pete and his classmates are excited.

The firehouse is huge! It's so big it can hold two long, red fire trucks and all of the firefighters' equipment.

The firefighters show the kids around.
They give everyone a turn to ring the old
brass fire bell outside the firehouse.

Then all the kids take turns sliding down the firefighters' pole.

"Wheeee!"

Callie yells as she glides down.

The firefighters allow the kids to try on their gear. Firefighters wear a lot of equipment.

First, Pete puts on the heavy black overalls.

Then he steps into the tall black boots.

A firefighter helps Pete put on the heavy yellow jacket.

Finally, they place a hard black helmet on Pete's head.

All this gear is very heavy. Pete can barely move!

The firefighters allow the kids to explore one of the fire trucks. Callie sits in the driver's seat. She presses the horn.

BRRRRRRRRT!

It's so loud that all the kids cover their ears.

Then Pete turns on the sirens and lights.
The sirens blare.

Wooo-eeeee! Wooo-eeeee!

The lights flash red and yellow.

Suddenly, a loud bell rings in the Firehouse. Uh oh! It's the fire alarm. There's a fire in town!

"Gear up, Pete!"

FIRE ALARM

The firefighters scramble into their gear very quickly. Pete puts on his gear, too.

They all climb aboard the fire truck and turn on the siren and lights. Firefighter Pete and the firefighters are on their way!

WooO-eeeee! WooO-eeeee!

The fire engine races through town
and the lights flash round and round.

There's the fire! It's hot and loud, but the firefighters know exactly what to do. They work together as a team to connect the fire truck to the fire hydrant.

Then the firefighters also attach a long, heavy hose to the truck. Firefighter Pete gives the signal and the firefighters turn on the water. Woosh!

The water gushes out very fast. Several firefighters must hold the hose to control it. Pete helps direct the hose as they spray the fire with water.

The fire is starting to go out. There is smoke everywhere.

Suddenly, Pete hears yelling from the roof.

Oh no! It's Grumpy Toad! He needs to be rescued.

The firefighters raise a long ladder from the truck.
Crank, crank, crank. The ladder goes up and up and up.

Firefighter Pete and another firefighter help Grumpy Toad climb down the ladder carefully. Yay! The fire is out and everyone is safe!

The firefighters drive back to the firehouse.
They take off all their gear.
They pat Pete on the back and say, "Good job, Pete!"
Firefighter Pete helped save the day!